I0867764

TEEN PROBLEMS

TEENS AND ANXIETY

By Tammy Gagne

ReferencePoint Press®

San Diego, CA

ReferencePoint Press®

© 2021 ReferencePoint Press, Inc.
Printed in the United States

For more information, contact:
ReferencePoint Press, Inc.
PO Box 27779
San Diego, CA 92198
www.ReferencePointPress.com

ALL RIGHTS RESERVED.

No part of this work covered by the copyright hereon may be reproduced or used in any form or by any means—graphic, electronic, or mechanical, including photocopying, recording, taping, web distribution, or information storage retrieval systems—without the written permission of the publisher.

Content Consultant: Carla Marie Manly, PhD

LIBRARY OF CONGRESS CATALOGING-IN-PUBLICATION DATA

Names: Gagne, Tammy, author.
Title: Teens and anxiety / by Tammy Gagne.
Description: San Diego : ReferencePoint Press, 2021. | Series: Teen problems | Includes bibliographical references and index. | Audience: Grades 10-12.
Identifiers: LCCN 2020003703 (print) | LCCN 2020003704 (eBook) | ISBN 9781682829578 (hardcover) | ISBN 9781682829585 (eBook)
Subjects: LCSH: Anxiety in adolescence--Juvenile literature. | Anxiety in adolescence--Treatment--Juvenile literature.
Classification: LCC BF724.3.A57 G34 2021 (print) | LCC BF724.3.A57 (eBook) | DDC 155.5/1246--dc23
LC record available at https://lccn.loc.gov/2020003703
LC eBook record available at https://lccn.loc.gov/2020003704

CONTENTS

INTRODUCTION

THE NAMELESS PROBLEM

Faith-Ann Bishop was an eighth grader in Bangor, Maine, when she began feeling anxious before school each day. The overwhelming fear that seemed to come out of nowhere often made her physically ill, sometimes even causing her to throw up. Many times she would decide to stay home instead of pushing through the anxiety to attend her classes. As much as she wanted to get up and go to school like everyone else, she found the task impossible some days. "It was like asking me to climb Mount Everest in high heels," she told journalist Susanna Schrobsdorff in an interview for *Time* magazine.[1]

Bishop did not fully understand what was happening to her. She knew she had a good life; as she saw it, she had no good reason to be so unhappy. For these reasons, Bishop decided not to tell her parents about what she was going through. Instead, she kept her feelings hidden as the problem worsened. She knew that her parents would listen and want to help her,

Anxiety disorders are the most common form of mental disorders in the United States. Anxiety disorders are more common in women, but men also experience anxiety.

but the idea of worrying them was too much for her to bear on top of her anxious feelings and the depression that soon accompanied them.

Bishop is one of many teens in the United States who have struggled with an anxiety disorder. As Schrobsdorff stated in *Time*, "It's a phenomenon that cuts across all demographics—suburban, urban, and rural; those who are college bound

> "It's a phenomenon that cuts across all demographics—suburban, urban, and rural; those who are college bound and those who aren't. Family financial stress can exacerbate these issues, and studies show that girls are more at risk than boys."[2]
>
> —*Susanna Schrobsdorff, journalist*

and those who aren't. Family financial stress can exacerbate these issues, and studies show that girls are more at risk than boys."[2]

Bishop eventually revealed what she was going through to her parents, who had suspected that something was wrong. They responded by seeking the psychotherapy their daughter needed to manage her anxiety and depression. She learned techniques for calming herself when her anxiety arose. Bishop also found a positive outlet for difficult emotions in Project Aware, a group that helps teens with anxiety and depression by teaching them how to make films. Bishop went on to write and direct a documentary about her mental health struggles called *The Road Back*. She found a support system in the people who helped work on the project. "I had a place where I could be open and talk about my life and the issues I was having, and then I could project them in an artistic way," Bishop said.[3]

Young people like Bishop often struggle to identify when anxiety has become a mental health problem. As psychiatrist Richard A. Friedman wrote in the *New York Times*, "There is a difference between an anxiety disorder and everyday anxiety.

It is normal for people to feel anxious before a big presentation or a test. But when these feelings become chronic, they could be a sign of an anxiety disorder.

The first impairs people's ability to function because they suffer from excessive anxiety even when there is little or nothing to be anxious about. The second is a perfectly normal and rational response to real stress. Teenagers—and people of all ages—will and *should* feel anxious occasionally."[4] When these feelings start escalating and become chronic, it is time to speak to a mental health professional.

CHAPTER ONE

WHAT IS TEEN ANXIETY?

Everyone experiences anxious feelings from time to time. Occasionally feeling anxious—nervous, uncertain, or uneasy—is a common and even healthy response to stress, especially for teenagers. Anxiety can sometimes lead a person to reexamine life choices. For example, feeling anxious can be a sign that a relationship isn't going well or that an extracurricular activity isn't the best match. In these cases, anxiety can lead to positive changes. Anxiety is also a common in the lead-up to high-stakes events, such as a big test or a playoff game. In these situations, feeling anxious can inspire a person to prepare and exert an abundance of effort. Anxiety can even serve as a warning system of sorts when something just doesn't feel right. When anxiety becomes intense or starts occurring frequently, however, it becomes more harmful than helpful.

Depression is another common mental disorder. Though depression is classified as a mood disorder and is separate from

Some anxiety before big events, such as a soccer game, can have positive effects. Anxiety might help players feel motivated or increase their alertness.

anxiety disorders, the two conditions often occur together. Major depressive disorder is characterized by persistent sadness and depressed mood occurring for at least two weeks, along with other symptoms such as fatigue, feelings of worthlessness, and a loss of interest in previously enjoyed activities.

The *Diagnostic and Statistical Manual of Mental Disorders* (*DSM*) is a book that categorizes mental health problems.

This is the first resource that most health care and mental health professionals, such as psychiatrists, psychologists, and counselors, turn to for diagnosing an anxiety disorder. The latest edition, the *DSM-5*, lists eleven different anxiety disorders. These include generalized anxiety disorder (GAD), social anxiety disorder, and separation anxiety disorder. Panic disorder is characterized by recurring, unexpected panic attacks. Another anxiety disorder is selective mutism. People with selective mutism disorder do not speak in certain situations, even though they do speak in other settings and are generally physically capable of doing so. Phobias, or extreme, irrational fears, are another anxiety disorder. Agoraphobia, or the fear of being in public spaces or crowds, is a separate anxiety disorder. Finally, the *DSM-5* includes substance/medication-induced anxiety disorder, anxiety disorder due to another medical condition, other specified anxiety disorder, and unspecified anxiety disorder. An anxiety disorder can cause a person to feel levels of anxiety disproportionate to the source of that anxiety. The exact cause of the anxiety, as well as the way that it presents itself, depends on the type of disorder, the symptoms, family history, and even the person experiencing it.

For a person with GAD, everyday routines—or just the thought of getting through a typical day—may cause anxious feelings. A person with GAD worries about multiple events, situations, or activities. Some people develop fears over their

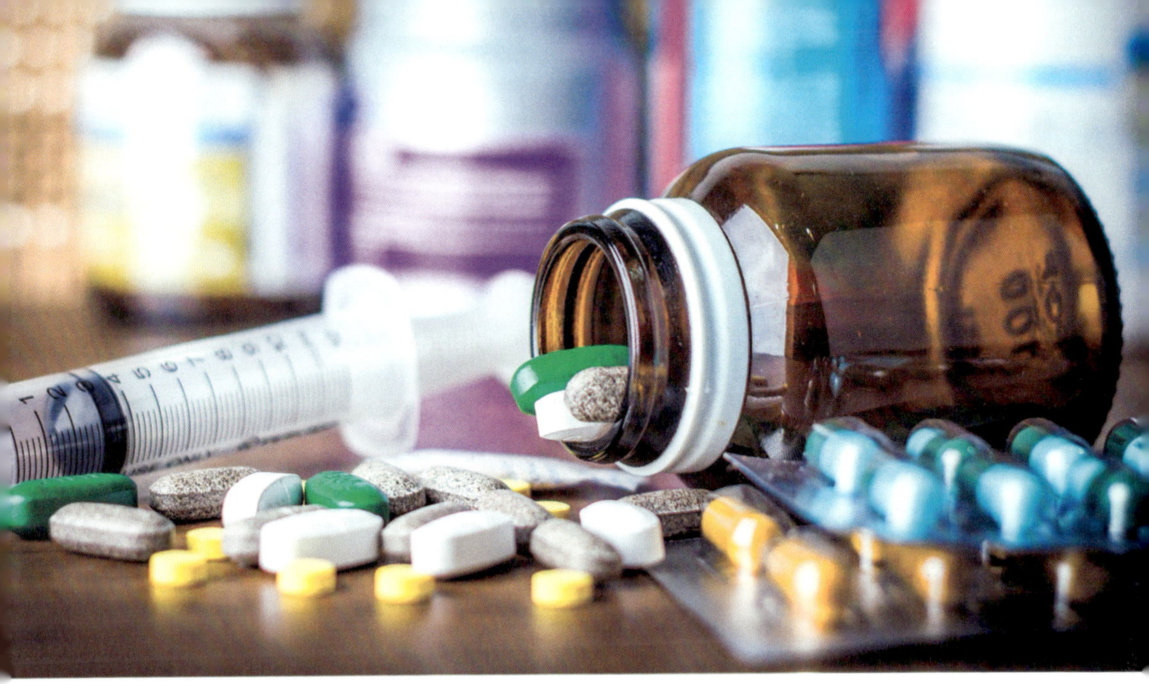

Some medications used to treat other health conditions have side effects that can cause anxiety. This can lead to a diagnosis of substance/medication-induced anxiety disorder.

health, even though there is no evidence of a physical problem. Although someone may realize that these feelings should not be as intense as they are, the person cannot control them. As the anxiety heightens, the person experiencing it finds it difficult to shift his or her focus away from worrying. Many people react by avoiding things that trigger the anxiety. Triggers are situations that can prompt anxious reactions. They can be isolated events, such as having to speak in public, or everyday events, such as going to school and visiting public places. Sometimes just the thought of fears can trigger an anxious response, even without a precipitating event taking place.

Separation anxiety disorder is more common in children than in adults. Younger teens may worry excessively about

Separation anxiety can keep teens from attending events such as sleepovers. While separation anxiety is most common in children, teens and adults can also experience it.

sleeping away from home. For some, an overnight school trip or an invitation to a sleepover can trigger massive anxiety. Kids with this problem may choose not to go, even if they would like to join in the fun. Some of these adolescents may also become attached to a parent or older sibling in a way that is not consistent with their age or cognitive development. Although they find the other person's presence comforting, the overdependence can become a problem for both parties.

The list of things that cause stress for teens is long. Many teens feel anxious about future events, but past behaviors can also keep a young person up at night. Teens commonly worry about social acceptance. Some young people may also stress over their personal abilities, family matters, or school performance. The weight of high expectations, whether coming from others or themselves, can be overwhelming for many teens. These worries can sometimes turn into social anxiety disorder. According to the *DSM-5*, social anxiety disorder includes "marked fear or anxiety about one or more social situations in which the individual is exposed to possible scrutiny by others. Examples include social interactions, . . . being observed, . . . and performing in front of others."[5]

In 2017, psychotherapist Amy Morin wrote an article for *Psychology Today* about the many reasons teens experience anxiety. "Some young people are overachieving perfectionists with a crippling fear of failure," she wrote. "Others worry so much about what their peers think of them that they're unable to function."[6] Morin added that superlative praise from parents, such as continually hearing that they are the best or the brightest, reinforces unrealistic expectations that teens may have for themselves.

> **"Some young people are overachieving perfectionists with a crippling fear of failure. Others worry so much about what their peers think of them that they're unable to function."[6]**
>
> ***—Amy Morin, psychotherapist***

Although anxiety can arise entirely on its own, it can also result as a secondary condition for someone dealing with another health problem. People who suffer from diabetes, heart disease, respiratory illnesses, and thyroid problems—conditions that affect the thyroid gland in the front of the neck—all face an increased risk of developing an anxiety disorder. People with chronic pain, regardless of its cause, are more prone to anxiety. Anxiety can also stem from substance abuse problems. Withdrawal from alcohol, for example, can lead to anxiety. Taking certain medications or stopping some medications too abruptly can also cause this problem. These are examples of substance/medication-induced anxiety disorder and anxiety disorder due to another medical condition.

WHO IS MOST AT RISK?

Several factors can contribute to whether a young person will develop an anxiety disorder. One factor is biology. Chemicals in the brain, such as norepinephrine and serotonin, work together to help control a person's mood and behavior. When an imbalance between these chemicals occurs, it affects a person's anxiety level. Although an imbalance of this sort is often inherited, it can also happen without any family history.

The environment in which a person lives can also prompt the development of anxiety. Children often grow up learning what to fear and how to react to those fears from their parents and other caregivers. If a parent is afraid of spiders, a child will likely be wary of them, too. Likewise, if the parent's fear is excessive, the

Pressure to do well in school can lead to feelings of anxiety. This pressure can be internal or come from others, such as parents.

child's may be as well. High parental expectations or an unstable home environment can also contribute to anxiety disorders.

Past experiences such as bullying can also contribute to the development of an anxiety disorder in a teen. In an article she wrote for the Verywell website, author and bullying prevention expert Sherri Gordon stated, "It is not uncommon for victims of bullying to worry or even expect that something bad is going to happen. After all, something bad *did* happen to them when they

> "It is not uncommon for victims of bullying to worry or even expect that something bad is going to happen. After all, something bad *did* happen to them when they were bullied. Consequently, this repeated stress can filter into other areas of their life and become a generalized anxiety disorder."[7]
>
> —***Sherri Gordon, author and bullying prevention expert***

were bullied. Consequently, this repeated stress can filter over into other areas of their life and become a generalized anxiety disorder."[7] In the case of experiencing or witnessing a severe trauma, such as a rape or other type of assault, a serious trauma disorder called post-traumatic stress disorder (PTSD) can result. A person with PTSD may be easily startled, irritable, or tense. She or he may also react intensely to these anxious feelings. A study published in the *Lancet Child and Adolescent Health* medical journal in 2018 reported that four out of five teenage girls who have been sexually assaulted will develop a mental health problem, such as anxiety or PTSD, in the months following the attack.

HOW COMMON ARE ANXIETY DISORDERS?

Anxiety is the most prevalent mental health disorder among children and adolescents. Nearly one in three adolescents will develop an anxiety disorder before the age of eighteen, with girls more likely to be diagnosed than boys. Experts point to several possible causes for the high ratio of adolescents with anxiety disorders. These include a culture obsessed with personal achievement, the pressures and constant presence of social media, and the rampant violence of terrorism and school shootings. Mental health professionals are also getting better at identifying anxiety and other mental health problems in youth, which may also play a role in higher numbers. Fear is sometimes at the heart of the problem. Many young people are afraid of letting their parents down, while other teens are afraid of not measuring up to their friends and fellow classmates. Many teens even fear simply spending time in public places because these spaces no longer feel safe to them. This is not always the case, though. Young people who rarely worry about how they are perceived by others can also develop anxiety.

RECLASSIFYING DISORDERS

As mental health professionals learn more about mental health disorders, the information in the *DSM* changes. For example, obsessive-compulsive disorder (OCD) and post-traumatic stress disorder (PTSD) were once considered types of anxiety disorders. The *DSM-5* added new classifications for these disorders. Although feelings of anxiety are part of OCD, the condition is now classified as a separate disorder. Likewise, PTSD is now considered a trauma disorder. The text even identifies a subtype of PTSD which is diagnosed in preschool children. The *DSM-5* also classified some disorders as anxiety disorders for the first time. Selective mutism disorder was one of these. Changes made to the *DSM* over time help caregivers provide the best possible treatment to people with each disorder.

Anxiety can have an escalating effect on a young person's routine and well-being. This was the case for a teenager named

THE PROBLEMS TEENS SEE

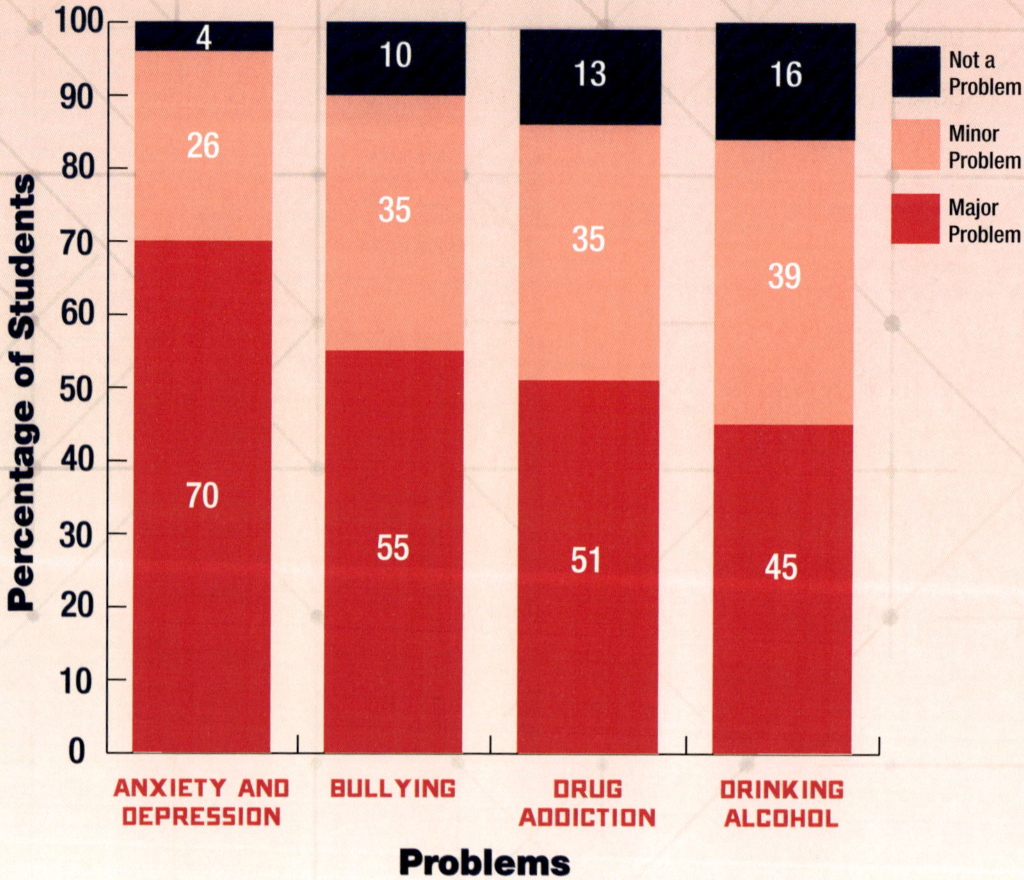

Source: Juliana Horowitz and Nikki Graf, "Most US Teens See Anxiety and Depression as a Major Problem Among Their Peers," Pew Research Center, *February 20, 2019. pewsocialtrends.org.*

The Pew Research Center surveyed teens in 2018. Teens were asked if they saw each of these issues as a major problem, a minor problem, or not a problem among their peers. Anxiety and depression topped the list of major problems. (The share of respondents who did not offer an answer is not shown.)

Jake, who shared his story in an interview with the *New York Times*. Jake was a good student and a talented athlete. To others he seemed fortunate, but deep down his biggest fear was failure, which was something he had never experienced. Jake's anxiety began with worries that he wouldn't get into a good college or succeed in life. He kept his fears to himself, but they soon became more than he could handle on his own. "You know how a normal person might have their stomach lurch if they walk into a classroom and there's a pop quiz? Well, I basically started having that feeling all the time."[8]

> "You know how a normal person might have their stomach lurch if they walk into a classroom and there's a pop quiz? Well, I basically started having that feeling all the time."[8]
>
> ***—Jake, a teen with anxiety***

Although his parents sought professional help for him when they realized what was happening, Jake's anxiety continued intensifying. Over the next year, he entered a vicious cycle of severe anxiety and depression. During one of his lowest points, he almost tried to take his own life. Desperate to improve the situation, Jake's parents decided to send him to a residential treatment center for teens with extreme anxiety. This type of facility treats patients for longer than the typical length of a hospital stay. Although outpatient treatment is far more common, patients who stay at a facility like this may remain there for weeks or sometimes even a few months. During Jake's two-month stay, he saw that

Having a support system is important for overcoming anxiety disorders. Group therapy can help teens with anxiety find support and understanding from other people experiencing similar issues.

he was far from alone in dealing with anxiety. Group therapy sessions at the facility were highly populated with other patients overwhelmed by their anxious feelings. By the time Jake left the program, he had made significant progress in learning to manage his anxiety. His new coping techniques helped him make it through his senior year. He was even accepted to his dream college.

THE STIGMA OF ANXIETY DISORDER

Part of what makes it difficult for many teens to admit that they are dealing with overwhelming anxiety is the stigma linked to it.

Mental health stigma is the negative association that other people attach to mental disorders, and it adds to the judgment a person with an anxiety disorder may already perceive from others. It is hard to manage feelings of not being good enough in some way if the act of seeking help for those feelings is considered a flaw or weakness.

Health care professionals sometimes prescribe medication for people with anxiety disorders. However, some people assume that people who take medication must be weak or not trying hard enough to get better on their own. Psychiatrist Sarper Taskiran says that this stigma often interferes with a patient's ability to get the help he or she needs. "Sadly, one of the most potent stigmas is against the use of sometimes lifesaving medications," Taskiran stated in a 2018 interview.[9] Antidepressants are a common medication to treat anxiety in teens. Taskiran cited a 2018 study showing that only 2.8 percent of adolescents receive prescriptions for antidepressants, even though the percentage of young people suffering from anxiety disorders is significantly higher than this.

One of the ways health care providers are working to reduce the stigma surrounding treatment for anxiety disorders is by making treatment options more prevalent in the places where young people live and learn. For example, more providers are utilizing technology to treat patients through the internet.

It is important to communicate with someone who is suffering from an anxiety disorder. Being supportive and understanding can help prevent symptoms from worsening.

Providing educators such as teachers, guidance counselors, and school nurses with information and training about helping young people manage anxiety problems can also help. As treatment becomes more commonplace, it will become more normal and acceptable to everyone. Some pediatricians are even embedding evaluation and treatment for anxiety issues into primary care services.

Although many young people with anxiety disorders fear being stigmatized, the increasing awareness and treatment of mental health issues have destigmatizing effects. Psychologist William Meek has treated many patients with anxiety disorders. He said, "Stigma is real and can certainly have an impact in some cases. However, for the overwhelming majority of people that I have worked with, stigma does not directly affect them. When they disclose their problems to close friends or family members, they often feel a dramatic enhancement of their relationships, not the exclusion or rejection that they fear."[10] Sharing one's feelings and experiences, whether positive or negative, can often bring people closer together. Family and friends who care can provide valuable emotional support to a person dealing with anxiety.

CHAPTER TWO

HOW DOES ANXIETY AFFECT TEENS?

Just the act of getting up each morning and following a typical high school routine can be challenging for some people with anxiety disorders. Whereas other teens might wake up looking forward to seeing friends at school or heading to a sports practice afterward, young people dealing with anxiety may feel dread instead. They might feel shortness of breath or even experience mild chest pain just thinking about all the things they have to do that day. Being able to adhere to a typical routine, however, does not mean that a teen isn't suffering from anxiety.

Of course, anyone may feel anxious about something like giving an oral report or trying out for a team, but for teens with an anxiety disorder, these feelings often aren't mild or fleeting. They cause distress or impairment and are persistent.

People suffering from an anxiety disorder respond strongly to stress. They have difficulty controlling their worries, which can interfere with their daily lives.

Dr. Stephen Carbone is a research and evaluation leader for Beyond Blue, a nonprofit organization in Australia that helps people with anxiety. Carbone explained how an anxiety disorder differs from more typical anxious feelings: "It is intense and severe and tends to impact your day-to-day functioning.

"[An anxiety disorder] is intense and severe and tends to impact your day-to-day functioning. Anxiety stops you from doing what you want to do and being who you want to be."[11]

—Dr. Stephen Carbone, research and evaluation leader for Beyond Blue

Anxiety stops you from doing what you want to do and being who you want to be."[11] People with anxiety disorders may also suffer with distress without experiencing impairment.

Someone with an anxiety disorder may realize that these feelings of anxiety are more intense than they should be, but knowing this does not make the feelings disappear or lessen. Chris Paine spoke about his experiences with anxiety with the Huffington Post. He developed anxiety even before he hit his teens, and the problem persisted for him into his twenties. He described his thought process as feeling like "every single fleeting thought you may have as a human being that raises the smallest bit of fear or doubt is red flagged in your brain—while all of the logical thoughts get thrown in the trash."[12]

Not everyone who has an anxiety disorder understands that it is beyond their control, however. Many teens dealing with anxiety disorders may worry that they simply aren't resilient enough. They may blame themselves when the problem is in fact a disorder that they have no more control over than a physical illness. Until they receive treatment that helps them manage their anxious feelings, the anxious feelings will likely continue or

Fear of rejection can make it difficult for someone with an anxiety disorder to make friends. People may avoid social gatherings because they are worried about the possibility of embarrassing themselves.

even intensify. Dealing with an anxiety disorder during the teen years can also be more challenging than during adulthood due to the added demands that academic and social pressures impose on young people. For example, young people may worry that if they do not take their academics seriously enough, they may never get into college.

WHAT HAPPENS IN THE BRAIN?

The human brain is a complex organ that controls nearly every aspect of a person's being. When a person perceives a threat, the brain evaluates the danger. When the threat is significant, the brain sends out an alert. Conversely, when the threat is small, the brain relays a message of calm. The brain of a person with an anxiety disorder does not handle this job properly, and without the brain's calming effect, the person experiences an amplified reaction to even a small threat.

Cognition, or learning, occurs in the frontal lobe. This part of the brain is also responsible for a person's rational thoughts. The amygdala, which is found deep inside the brain, is responsible for a person's emotional processing. The amygdala may cause a person to feel scared when riding in an elevator, but the frontal lobe will reassure that person that everything will be fine. It understands the rational idea that millions of people use elevators safely each day. This lessens the person's fear and makes it more manageable. Anxiety causes the emotional part of the brain to overpower the cognitive part. For example, when a person with claustrophobia—an irrational fear of enclosed spaces—encounters an elevator, the fear-based part of the brain typically wins out.

Scientists are still learning about the long-term effects of anxiety on the brain. One study conducted in 2016 found that extreme forms of anxiety can actually damage the brain. Clinical scientist Linda Mah, who led the study, explained, "Pathological anxiety and chronic stress are associated with structural

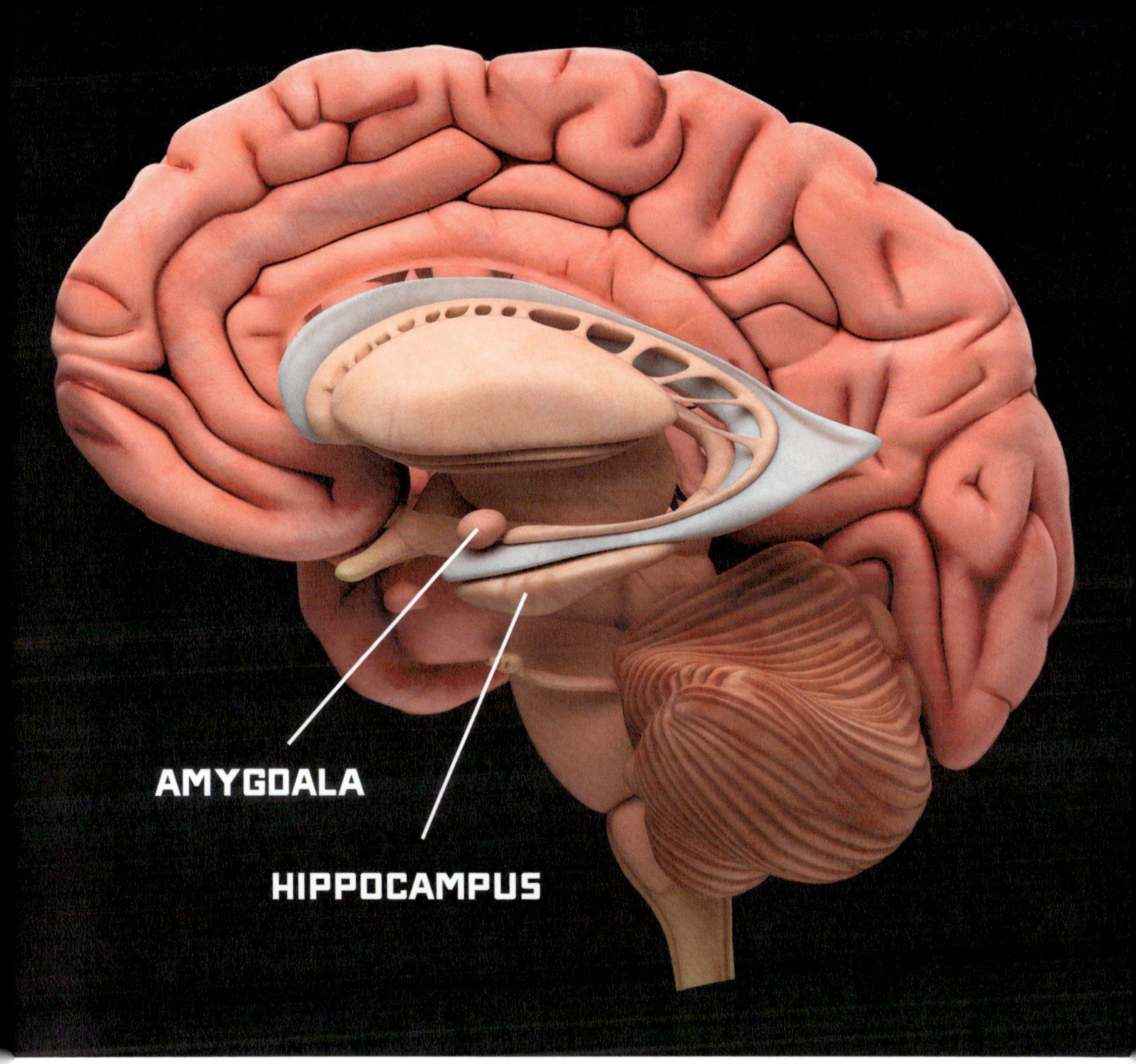

Anxiety has been linked to activity in the brain. The amygdala, which responds to fear, is overactive in those who experience excessive anxiety.

degeneration and impaired functioning of the hippocampus."[13] This means that certain areas of the brain deteriorate or stop working properly. The hippocampus is a part of the brain that plays an important a role in the consolidation of memories. Mah's study found a strong link between anxiety disorders and Alzheimer's disease—an illness that causes memory loss—as well as depression.

Another study found that improving cognition by training the brain to perform better can also reduce the occurrence of anxiety, even when an imbalance is present. Professor Ahmad Hariri, who led this study, explained that when brain functioning in the frontal lobe is higher, "the imbalance in these deeper brain structures is not expressed as changes in mood or anxiety."[14]

HOW A PANIC ATTACK LOOKS TO OTHERS

Seeing someone experience a panic attack is neither pleasant nor easy. Although it may be difficult to stand by and feel powerless to help, it's important not to aggravate the situation by overreacting. Experts recommend that witnesses to a panic attack remind the person having the attack to breathe regularly. Taking deep breaths—in for four seconds, then out for an additional four—can be calming for many people. It may also be helpful to reassure the person that the situation is only temporary. Telling the person to calm down, however, is rarely helpful. Instead, mental health professionals recommend staying with the person until the attack has passed. Most importantly, they say, don't act annoyed or judgmental.

EFFECTS ON THE BODY

Anxiety is an emotional response to fear that can also manifest in a myriad of physical ways. In addition to the intense fear a person with anxiety may feel, he or she may also experience breathing problems, a pounding heart, nausea, or diarrhea. Some people also suffer from headaches. Anxiety can raise a person's blood pressure, cause fatigue, or even lead to muscle aches or other physical pains.

Sometimes people with anxiety disorders experience panic attacks. According to the *DSM-5*, "A panic attack is an abrupt surge of intense fear or intense discomfort that reaches a peak within minutes, and during which time four (or more)" symptoms from a list of thirteen are present.[15] These symptoms include pounding heart, sweating, shaking, chest pain, and fear of dying. Panic attacks can occur both when a person is feeling calm and when a person is feeling anxious. The physical symptoms of a panic attack can feel so severe that people mistake it for a heart attack. If panic attacks occur with enough frequency, the sufferer could be diagnosed with panic disorder. When someone experiences panic attacks but does not meet the criteria for a panic disorder diagnosis, a panic attack specifier may be

ANXIETY ATTACKS VS. PANIC ATTACKS

What is the difference between panic and anxiety attacks? Though the two terms sound alike, they do not mean the same thing. According to clinical professional counselor Sheryl Ankrom, "'Anxiety attack' is not a formal, clinical term, but one that is used by many people to describe all sorts of things, from feeling worried about an upcoming event to intense feelings of terror or fear that would meet the diagnostic criteria for a panic attack." Panic attacks are outlined in the *DSM-5*, with specific criteria for diagnosis. *Panic attack* is a clinical term. People should be careful to use accurate language when discussing anxiety disorders, and avoid saying *anxiety attack* when they really mean *panic attack*.

Sheryl Ankrom, "Emotions During an Anxiety Attack," Verywell Mind, *March 23, 2020. www.verywellmind.com.*

added to his or her other diagnoses. Some people with anxiety disorders will never experience a panic attack.

Ongoing anxiety can cause other physical responses within the body. When a person feels anxious, the brain releases stress hormones, such as adrenaline and cortisol. Although these hormones help a person manage short-term stress, when they are released too often, they can increase the chances that the person will experience headaches, dizziness, or even depression.

OTHER EFFECTS OF ANXIETY

One of the most difficult parts of having an anxiety disorder is that people do not always know what causes the anxiety. For some people, this seemingly random aspect of the problem can make it even more frightening. A young woman named Desirae shared her personal story on the National Alliance of Mental Illness (NAMI) website. She wanted others to understand how an anxiety disorder feels. "Just imagine yourself doing daily routines and out of nowhere you feel panicky, anxious, your heart starts to race and you don't know what triggered it and don't know when it's going to stop," Desirae wrote.[16] She went on to explain that at these times,

> **"Just imagine yourself doing daily routines and out of nowhere you feel panicky, anxious, your heart starts to race and you don't know what triggered it and don't know when it's going to stop."[16]**
>
> ***—Desirae, a young woman with an anxiety disorder***

Some people with anxiety disorders experience panic attacks. Symptoms of panic attacks include sweating, pounding heart, and chest pain.

she also worries about what her anxiety looks like to others. For people with anxiety disorders, the worry becomes a vicious cycle. Desirae even worried that her explanation of anxiety sounded silly to those who would read it.

Worrying about what others may think can lead a person with an anxiety disorder to become more socially isolated. This can also turn into a problematic cycle, especially in the case of social anxiety. When anxiety stems from worrying about

Anxiety disorders and depression commonly occur together. Some antidepressants can be used to treat both anxiety and depression.

how one is viewed by peers, feeling shunned or alone can increase the risk of developing a secondary condition, such as depression. Spending too much time alone can quickly lead anxious teens to feeling a decrease in their self-worth, which then makes them feel even more anxious about spending time with others.

Although they are two separate conditions, many young people suffer from both anxiety and depression. This does not mean that a person with anxiety will always develop depression, but there is enough overlap between the two problems to lead caregivers to think that treatment for anxiety might help prevent depression. Some studies show that 60 percent of people with anxiety disorders also show symptoms of depression.

For many teens, the worst possible time for a panic attack to strike is when they are at school among their peers. Salli-Ann Holloway learned what this felt like when she was in high school. When she began gasping for air during class, she headed to the nurse's office. Holloway's anxiety was interrupting her education. She was a bright student who had earned her entrance into high-level classes, but living up to the expectations of such classes was intensifying her anxiety. In an interview with the *Atlantic*, she shared, "A lot of people always say junior year is the hardest. With people telling me that, it got me in that mindset, and I was taking challenging classes. It was definitely a year when everybody did a lot of growing up and so a lot of things changed

> "A lot of people always say junior year is the hardest. With people telling me that, it got me in that mindset, and I was taking challenging classes. It was definitely a year when everybody did a lot of growing up and so a lot of things changed with your friendships, the classes and thinking about the future more than we've ever had to. That all just contributed and made it worse."[17]
>
> ***—Salli-Ann Holloway, on her anxiety***

Avoiding triggers for anxiety is only a short-term solution. Someone who is suffering from an anxiety disorder should work with a mental health professional to develop healthy coping strategies.

with your friendships, the classes and thinking about the future more than we've ever had to. That all just contributed and made it worse."[17]

One might assume that the best thing to do for a person in the midst of a panic attack is to provide comfort and remove the trigger. Providing comfort is important, but shielding the person from everyday situations that cause anxiety can actually worsen the anxiety. A well-intended person can lead the anxiety sufferer to become too dependent on this short-term solution, therefore enabling him or her instead of helping to solve the problem.

Simply avoiding triggers can be both ineffective and impractical, but learning to manage the anxiety can make a big difference. Holloway's school nurse helped her breathe through each attack, so she could return to class instead of leaving school for the rest of the day.

Although many teens face anxiety disorders, a diagnosis does not have to be a precursor to a lifetime of overwhelming feelings. In fact, seeking treatment for the disorder can help people who suffer from it learn to manage the anxiety so it doesn't become the focal point of their lives. The sooner people seek treatment, the sooner they can get back to enjoying more of their time.

CHAPTER THREE

HOW DOES TEEN ANXIETY AFFECT SOCIETY?

People who know and care about a person with an anxiety disorder may want to help, but knowing what is and isn't helpful can be challenging. Some people assume that the best way to lessen a person's anxiety is by dismissing it. These people may try to reassure a friend with anxiety that there is nothing to worry about. Some people try to help by ignoring the anxiety altogether, as if acknowledging it will make the situation worse. Sometimes family members or close friends even lie to others, trying to pass the anxiety off as something else in an effort to save the sufferer embarrassment. None of these approaches usually helps.

Anyone can suffer from anxiety. Bojan Krkic is a Spanish athlete known for his exceptional abilities on the soccer field.

Bojan Krkic and other celebrities have begun speaking out about their experiences with anxiety. Conversation about mental health is important in reducing stigma.

At just seventeen years old, Krkic was offered the opportunity to play at the professional level in Barcelona. The pressures of becoming a professional player led Krkic to suffer from debilitating anxiety. Like other popular athletes, soccer players face enormous scrutiny from social media. They become targets on Twitter and other social media platforms, where fans turn criticizing players into a sport of its own. Commentary often turns hateful. Although Krkic knew that he shouldn't let mean comments affect him, it was hard for him to ignore them.

For Krkic, the problem became a daily struggle. "Anxiety affects everyone differently," he told the *Guardian* years later. "I spoke to someone who felt like their heart was beating 1,000 times a minute. With me, it was a dizziness, feeling sick, constant, 24 hours a day."[18]

Before games, Krkic found himself stuck in the locker room, unable to take the field due to his panic attacks. The team officials did not know how to explain Krkic's absence to fans. "[T]here are lots of things that people don't know," Krkic confided. "I didn't go to the [2008] European Championship because of anxiety issues but we said I was going on holiday. I was called up for Spain against France, my international debut, and it was said that I had gastroenteritis when I had [a panic attack]. But no one wants to talk about that. [Soccer's] not interested."[19]

> **"[T]here are lots of things that people don't know. I didn't go to the [2008] European Championship because of anxiety issues but we said I was going on holiday. . . . But no one wants to talk about that. [Soccer's] not interested."[19]**
>
> ***—Bojan Krkic, Spanish soccer star***

A young person does not need to be famous or a high achiever to suffer from anxiety. Any child or adolescent can develop an anxiety disorder, but some factors make kids even more susceptible to this problem. Those who grow up in poverty, for example, have higher rates of both anxiety and depression. A large number of young people with

Certain populations have a higher risk of developing an anxiety disorder than others. For example, immigrants may have difficulties adjusting to a new environment, which can cause anxiety.

anxiety also have a history of early life trauma. This can include abuse, neglect, or the loss of a parent. In addition to increasing the chance that a young person will develop anxiety, early life trauma can also worsen anxiety that the person may suffer much later in life.

Anxiety does not discriminate. It affects young people of different races, genders, and sexual identities. The symptoms of anxiety are no different, but adolescents from minority backgrounds often experience added stressors—such as racism or bullying—that can add to the problem. These factors can intensify the anxiety experienced by a young person of color or lesbian, gay, bisexual, transgender, or queer/questioning (LGBTQ) youth.

SOCIETY'S VIEW OF ANXIETY

Many people in today's society who do not suffer from an anxiety disorder use the words *stress* and *anxiety* interchangeably. Others might assume that a person experiencing anxiety is seeking attention, exaggerating, or even making up the anxiety. They might belittle the person or accuse him or her of trying to use anxiety as an excuse to get out of a responsibility, such as going to school.

Some people may have a hard time believing that a person's anxiety is real because they do not understand or relate to the experience themselves. To people who have never suffered from this problem personally, anxiety may seem like an overreaction to minor stress. It can be difficult for these people to understand that anxiety can occur even when there is no apparent trigger.

It is common for critics of anxiety disorders to put their own labels on the problem. Some even offer advice to the sufferer, even though they have no mental health training. Male teens with anxiety often hear from these critics that they just need to

People with anxiety disorders may experience stigma. People who don't have anxiety may not understand the level of distress caused by an anxiety disorder and think the sufferer is simply seeking attention.

be tougher. Freelance writer Saim Cheeda has dealt with anxiety since he was a teen. Cheeda called this the "man-up response." He said, "This does nothing for the person suffering from anxiety, as the advice offers nothing of substance. Adverse effects of shutting down fears rather than confronting them can result in a false idea of masculinity and prolonging the issue of anxiety."[20]

Critics may also accuse a person with anxiety of being arrogant. Many people with social anxiety disorder avoid social situations because they find them too triggering. Others who are

Some people believe that constant comparisons and social media are responsible for rising numbers of teens with anxiety. While technology can help people in some ways, it can have a negative impact on mental health.

more social mistake this avoidance as snobbery. The way they see it, the person with the anxiety thinks he or she is somehow better than everyone else, but in many cases nothing could be further from the truth. Those who suffer from anxiety often withdraw because they are immobilized by fear.

Of course, not everyone in society dismisses anxiety as an attention-seeking act or a problem that can be quickly solved with a little more mental strength. People do not have to have firsthand experience to be sensitive to the struggles of others. Many people for whom anxiety has never been a problem are nonetheless respectful and understanding to those with an anxiety disorder. These people can make a big difference to a person dealing with this condition. The genuine support of family members and friends can help a person in the midst of learning how to cope with anxiety.

IS SOCIETY TO BLAME FOR ANXIETY DISORDERS?

Many mental health professionals think modern society is at least partially responsible for the growing number of people suffering from anxiety. Technology, especially in Western culture, has changed dramatically in the twenty-first century, with electronics and other machines shifting society's focus. Young people used to spend the majority of their free time with family or friends in person. In 2018, 89 percent of teens owned a smartphone. On average, teens spend more than seven hours each day using smartphones, according to a 2019 study by Common Sense Media. While technology itself is not problematic, misuse and overuse can create significant mental health effects.

Social media platforms expose users to constant comparisons to other users. Young people frequently post selfies to apps such as Instagram and Snapchat using the most

SOCIAL MEDIA CAN TRIGGER ANXIETY

Digital technology has become a huge part of teens' daily lives. Parents and other adults have become concerned about how devices such as smartphones and tablets may be affecting teens' mental health. Part of the problem is balancing the real world and its sometimes-disappointing experiences with the pressure for everything to seem ideal online. Young people who already suffer from a mental disorder are especially vulnerable; they are even more likely than the average teen to visit multiple social media platforms regularly. Experts say this habit often stems from the fear of missing out, or FOMO. Being active online often makes teens feel like they are being included, something they may not feel from their real-life relationships. Young people also succumb to great pressure to look as good as possible, even if this means manipulating their images to look like completely different people. All this pressure and worry can understandably lead to heightened anxiety. At the same time, some teens find that the connections they maintain online help to reduce their stress. For these teens, electronic devices may decrease anxiety. Finding balance allows social media to become one part of a teen's healthy lifestyle and interpersonal relationships.

flattering photo filters. They share updates about the most enviable parts of their lives; few people want to show themselves in a bad light, either literally or figuratively. All this effort at creating an appealing online image can take its toll on teens using social media, especially those with an anxiety disorder. Seeing their peers posting about invitations to homecoming dances or extravagant birthday gifts from parents can make young people with anxiety feel like they aren't good enough. They often do not understand that they are comparing themselves, viewed through the critical filter of their fears and insecurities, with idealized versions of their peers' lives. Even some of the most seemingly popular or happy young people may feel like they fall short of the other people they follow on social media. It can become a constant game of trying to keep up.

Teens with anxiety often read more into a situation than is reasonable or intended, both in real life and in their virtual spaces. For example, when these young people post on social media about their own lives, they may focus too much on a single negative comment. They may even worry that positive comments are meant in a bad way. When something good happens, and a friend says, "Good for you!" or "Wow!," teens with anxiety might convince themselves that the person is being sarcastic. According to psychologist Marwa Azab, "The number of things that might be interpreted as negative by non-anxious people is significantly less than an anxious person. So, an anxious person might interpret most neutral events/comments as negative. If a word has multiple meanings, they will likely choose the most negative meaning."[21]

> **"The number of things that might be interpreted as negative by non-anxious people is significantly less than an anxious person. So, an anxious person might interpret most neutral events/comments as negative. If a word has multiple meanings, they will likely choose the most negative meaning."[21]**
>
> ***—Marwa Azab, psychologist***

Society's emphasis on material success can play a role in this worry and envy as much as good looks and

Teenagers and young adults who spend a lot of time on social media may constantly compare their lives to the lives of others. They may worry that their lives are less interesting than the lives of their peers.

popularity can. The link between focusing on material success and the development of anxiety isn't new. A study conducted in the 1990s showed that people whose biggest goals involved their appearance, income, and status were more likely to suffer from anxiety and depression. The typical goals of young people today indicate that many teens could be headed for an anxious future. More than half of teens polled by Pew Research Center in 2019 reported that money would be either "important" or "very important" to them in their futures.

This intense focus on achieving material success can actually detract from a healthy support system for someone battling anxiety. Promises Behavior Health is a mental health treatment center in Brentwood, Tennessee. A blog article on the facility's website explains that many teens blame cultural changes for the rise in anxiety among their age group: "They say that our society's increasing materialism over the years has eroded personal relationships and families. We now value money and personal luxuries more than relationships."[22]

SPEAKING OPENLY ABOUT ANXIETY

Support for dealing with anxiety disorders can come from a variety of people. Once a person has been diagnosed with an anxiety disorder, a mental health care provider and the patient will agree on a treatment plan. As the patient goes through this process, a support system can be invaluable. Knowing that others want to be helpful can ease some of the stress of accepting the diagnosis and implementing the changes necessary to manage it. Feeling accepted and supported can help ease feelings of embarrassment that can compound anxiety. If others are critical, the anxiety can worsen before it gets better.

Some family doctors have started screening for symptoms of depression and anxiety in their patients. This was how a young

Conversations about mental health are not always easy, but communication and support can make living with an anxiety disorder easier. A strong support system of trusted friends who are willing to listen can help reduce feelings of isolation.

woman from Wisconsin named Cady first became aware of her anxiety. She had recently started attending a new middle school, and this change in her routine triggered some anxious feelings. Although she didn't know how to name these feelings at that time, she needed some support in dealing with them. After reading Cady's depression screening form at her annual checkup, Cady's pediatrician realized she might be suffering from both anxiety and depression.

Cady's treatment program utilized talk therapy, which is a psychotherapeutic treatment centered on conversations with a mental health professional. Treatment helped her learn to calm herself when her anxious feelings rose up or intensified. In her case, the simple fact that she had a mental health disorder became something that she could tell herself in difficult moments. This made her feelings more manageable. But Cady soon noticed that not everyone was as comfortable discussing mental health issues as she was. When she graduated from eighth grade, each student needed to deliver a speech at the ceremony on a topic of his or her choice. Cady chose to talk to the audience about her anxiety. "I wanted to talk about it, because it seemed like no one else was. People don't like to admit that mental health is a taboo subject," she said, "but it is."[23]

She wanted to make sure that other young people with anxiety understood that having an anxiety disorder does not mean that there is something wrong with them. She explained in her speech that anxiety is just a condition that some people have. By talking about the problem openly, she hoped to help eliminate the embarrassment that others with the condition may feel.

Society can make it difficult for people with anxiety or another mental health issue to speak frankly about their disorders. Most people easily accept and sympathize with signs of illness or injury they can see—a head left hairless from recent cancer treatment, a broken arm or leg in a cast, or even a runny nose turned red from the common cold. People typically rally around people with life-threatening diseases. They open doors or carry bags for people with broken bones, and they bring get-well soup to friends with the flu.

Unfortunately, those with mental health disorders are often not given the same consideration. Anxiety cannot be seen by others at a glance. In fact, many people with anxiety often do their best to hide it, fearing society's reaction. Clare Allan is an author who writes about mental health issues. She discussed this problem in an article for the *Guardian*: "For many people, it is hard to accept that severe anxiety, for example, might incapacitate someone from leaving their house as genuinely as if they were suffering from a physical paralysis. The fact that the problem cannot be seen makes it easier to dismiss."[24] Although Allan and many others are trying to change society's perception of and response

"For many people, it is hard to accept that severe anxiety, for example, might incapacitate someone from leaving their house as genuinely as if they were suffering from a physical paralysis. The fact that the problem cannot be seen makes it easier to dismiss."[24]

—Clare Allan, writer specializing in mental health issues

Conversations about mental health are important. They allow people to become more understanding and compassionate toward those with a mental disorder.

to mental illness, she admits that even she has told others she was suffering from a migraine when in fact it was her anxiety that was making it too difficult to take part in a planned activity.

Allan knows firsthand that not having her anxiety on display for the rest of the world can make things easier sometimes, but she also knows that its invisibility can make the disorder more isolating. "[T]he more we hide our difficulties," she wrote, "the more invisible they, and we, become."[25]

CHAPTER FOUR

HOW CAN WE TREAT AND PREVENT TEEN ANXIETY?

Just as the symptoms and causes of anxiety can vary, the method chosen to treat an anxiety disorder depends on many factors. The types of symptoms patients are experiencing, their triggers, and their personal preferences play a role in deciding what form of treatment might work best for them. It is also important to consider whether any other mental health issues could be part of the problem. For example, for a patient with both anxiety and depression, a medication that can improve both these issues might be ideal. Counseling, medication, or a combination of these two types of treatment can be helpful if anxiety becomes too much for a person to handle.

Anxiety disorders are diagnosed by mental health professionals. Primary care doctors and psychiatrists may also prescribe medication that can treat anxiety.

MENTAL HEALTH ASSESSMENT

When it comes to seeking an assessment from a health care provider, teens who think they may have an anxiety disorder have a variety of options. They can start the process by speaking with a primary care doctor, who can then provide a referral to a mental health professional if needed. Although primary care physicians do not typically offer therapy, some will treat anxiety by prescribing medications, or they might write a prescription to help ease symptoms until a patient can find a therapist.

Some people choose to work with psychiatrists, who often provide both psychotherapy and medication. Many people also choose to start treatment by consulting with a psychotherapist, such as a psychologist or other mental health provider.

Because anxiety can manifest in many forms with different causes, diagnosing an anxiety disorder isn't a quick or simple task. Although mental health conditions are just as real and serious as physical afflictions, mental health care providers rarely have physical tests such as blood tests to diagnose the problems they treat. Instead, they must conduct diagnostic interviews and carefully interpret a patient's responses and behavior. Before they can do that, however, the best approach is beginning with a full medical history, including all medications the patient is currently taking, and a complete physical examination. This is another reason that an appointment with a primary care doctor can be an excellent starting point. This doctor can help rule out a physical problem that could be playing a role in the anxious feelings.

It can be difficult to talk to a stranger or even an acquaintance such as a primary care doctor about anxious feelings, especially if it is the first time the patient has done so. But it is extremely important that he or she be honest and thorough during the assessment. Sometimes anxiety symptoms appear as a result of substance abuse. If the young person has been drinking alcohol or taking nonprescription drugs, the doctor needs this information for an accurate diagnosis.

For some teens, seeking a diagnosis and starting treatment are difficult steps. Sometimes fear of stigma or the possible side effects of medication cause people to put off seeking help. This was the case for Nancy, a teen from New York whose undiagnosed anxiety led to suicidal ideation. In a letter she sent to the *New York Times*, she shared, "I finally went to my general physician and was told it was an effect of anxiety, so I went to a neurologist to get a second opinion and was told the same thing. I refused to accept the diagnosis at first—I remember saying to a friend that I wish the doctor had told me I had a brain tumor instead. Neurosurgery was a more appealing prospect to me than

CONTINUING ANXIETY INTO ADULTHOOD

Although some young people might convince themselves that they can manage their anxiety on their own, refusing to seek professional help can increase the chances that anxiety will become a problem well past the teen years. Anxiety sufferers who choose to go it alone also raise the risk of their symptoms worsening, as well as their risk for developing other mental health problems as they get older. As their friends are graduating from high school and deciding which colleges they will attend, young people with severe anxiety have higher rates of dropping out of school. Many also have a hard time transitioning into adulthood. They may be unable to hold down a job or even be afraid to move out of their parents' homes. What begins as a minor mental health problem can end up affecting a person's entire future when he or she avoids acknowledging the problem and learning how to cope with it.

Therapy and other treatments for anxiety disorders have proven to be very effective. However, less than 50 percent of people diagnosed with an anxiety disorder receive treatment.

therapy and medication."[26] Eventually, though, Nancy began to feel hopeful about her treatment. She even reached the point of wishing she had sought treatment sooner.

There are many treatment options available to people with anxiety disorders. No two treatment plans will look exactly alike. However, many treatment plans utilize psychotherapy, medication, or a combination of the two.

COGNITIVE BEHAVIORAL THERAPY (CBT)

Most often, counseling focuses on cognitive behavioral therapy (CBT), which aims to change the way people think when they feel anxious by changing how they respond to these feelings. Many teens with anxiety suffer from distorted thinking, meaning they distort, or twist, information from their environment. The negative thought patterns that result from this way of thinking can heighten anxiety. Jerry Bubrick is a clinical psychologist who treats young people with anxiety disorders. In an article he wrote for the Child Mind Institute website, he explained, "Cognitive behavioral therapy is based on the idea that how we think and act both affect how we feel. By changing thinking that is distorted, and behavior that is dysfunctional, we change our emotions."[27] Exposure therapy, which involves confronting the situations that typically trigger anxiety, is also an important part of CBT. Its objective is to reduce anxiety through repeated exposure.

"Cognitive behavioral therapy is based on the idea that how we think and act both affect how we feel. By changing thinking that is distorted, and behavior that is dysfunctional, we change our emotions."[27]

—Clinical psychologist Jerry Bubrick, who treats young people with anxiety disorders

Negative thoughts are usually at the root of anxiety. Replacing those worrisome thoughts with more positive ones can lessen the hold anxiety exerts over a person through fear.

Someone suffering from an anxiety disorder may spiral into negative thinking. Cognitive behavioral therapy helps people change their thought processes.

After exploring a patient's most common anxiety triggers in therapy, a mental health care provider will help him or her construct a plan for coping when anxiety strikes. More than twenty years of research has shown that CBT—especially when it includes exposure therapy—is the most effective therapeutic treatment for anxiety.

MEDICATIONS FOR TREATING ANXIETY

A variety of medications can also help reduce the symptoms of an anxiety disorder. Researchers found that some antidepressants (selective serotonin reuptake inhibitors, or SSRIs) were also effective in treating anxiety. These include Prozac, Lexapro, and Zoloft. These medications increase levels of a brain chemical called serotonin. Side effects can include nausea and insomnia.

Some medications used to treat anxiety for adults have not been specifically tested in children and teens. Blood pressure medications called beta-blockers can help reduce physical symptoms of anxiety, such as heart palpitations, shaking, and sweating. They may be prescribed for teens with social anxiety.

Buspirone is part of a class of medications called anxiolytics. It can also be used to treat anxiety in adults. However, a 2017 study found that buspirone had no noticeable effect on GAD in adolescent patients compared to a placebo.

Benzodiazepines are another type of anxiolytic. These include Xanax and Klonopin. Benzodiazepines are often used to treat anxiety in adults. However, this class of drugs can be addictive. Most doctors tend to use them only temporarily and as a last resort, especially for patients who have a history of substance abuse. Benzodiazepines have not been proven effective in children and teens. Because of this and their addictive nature, doctors do not recommend using benzodiazepines for children and teens with anxiety.

No single medication is right for everyone. Most people must go through a trial-and-error approach with their health care professional to see which drug or dosage works best for

Medications can be prescribed to help treat anxiety. Because responses to medications can vary, people should only take prescribed medication as directed by a health care professional.

them. Although this process can take some time, finding the right match for one's body chemistry can make a significant difference. Many medications also have side effects. Doctors and patients must weigh the benefits and liabilities of each medication in deciding if it is the best course of action. People should only take prescribed medication as directed. They should never experiment with dosage or try someone else's medication.

A Washington teen named Alex said that she refused to take medication to treat her anxiety for years. She worried about what others would think of her if they learned that she was taking medication. Although it took time for her mental health care providers to find the best medication for her, Alex saw the difference that medication and therapy ultimately made in her life. This helped her let go of her worries about others' opinions. "Having anxiety doesn't define me, nor should it define anyone else."[28]

> "Having anxiety doesn't define me, nor should it define anyone else."[28]
>
> *—Alex, a teen with an anxiety disorder*

OTHER WAYS TO MANAGE ANXIETY

Teaching anxiety sufferers to manage stress can help them calm themselves when anxious feelings arise. Relaxation techniques and other mental exercises can interrupt feelings of anxiety when these exercises are performed regularly or before anticipated triggers. Physical exercise and a healthy diet can also reduce anxiety for many people.

Some schools are incorporating mindfulness classes into their curriculum to help students deal with stress and anxiety. One such school is Wilson High School in Portland, Oregon. Cassia McIntyre was a junior at the school when she took the mindfulness class. She told the *Washington Post*, "Sometimes I have trouble breathing; I have panic attacks. This class helps me bring more attention to my breath and overcome that. I'm less stressed-out and able to better cope with stress."[29] While these self-help strategies alone are not enough to combat anxiety, they can be used in conjunction with therapy and medication to manage symptoms.

PREVENTING ANXIETY

Because anxiety disorders have become so common, learning about how to prevent them is a smart step for young people who have a high amount of stress in their lives. Feeling pressure to succeed academically, navigating the demanding circles of adolescent social life, and managing the arrival of hormones that course through a teenage body can all lead to anxious feelings. Knowing how to handle those feelings can often keep them from escalating into an anxiety disorder.

Just as certain behaviors can help a person manage anxiety, some types of behavior can also help prevent it. Eating a healthy diet and getting plenty of physical exercise are especially important. When stress starts to build up, working out or playing a sport can help relieve tension. Exercise can also improve someone's mood by prompting his or her body to produce endorphins. Endorphins are natural chemicals that reduce pain, increase immunity to illnesses, and generally help a person relax.

Establishing a self-care routine can help manage symptoms of anxiety. Exercise and other hobbies help reduce stress.

A study that surveyed more than 1 million Americans found that people who exercise have fewer poor mental health days than people who do not exercise. Lakshmy Nair discussed this study in a 2018 article for the Livestrong website. She stated, "Of the 75 activities recorded, the researchers found that team sports, cycling, and aerobic and gym activities made the biggest difference."[30]

Getting enough sleep can also help prevent anxiety from becoming a problem. According to Harvard Medical School, insomnia—the inability to sleep—may be a risk factor for anxiety disorders, but researchers are uncertain about which condition causes the other. People who tend to sleep poorly have an increased risk of developing anxiety, and people with anxiety disorders often have a hard time falling asleep at night. Insomnia can also worsen the symptoms of anxiety. For all these reasons, it is best to create a healthy sleep routine before a problem arises. Going to bed at the same time each night and getting up at the same time each day can help, as can avoiding electronic screens in the two hours before bedtime. Silencing or turning off phones at night can help prevent disrupted sleep that occurs from receiving text messages in the night.

THE PROGNOSIS FOR ANXIETY DISORDERS

Anxiety disorders are highly treatable, but how successful treatment is depends on many factors. These include the exact form of anxiety experienced, its severity, whether other mental health conditions are present, and the type of treatment used. The one thing that is almost certain is that, if left untreated, an anxiety disorder will likely get worse. This is why it is so important to seek help for anxiety as soon as possible. If not given appropriate treatment, an anxiety disorder in a teen can impair the young person's family life, friendships, school

People can learn to manage their anxiety symptoms with treatment. Then they will be better prepared to handle days when their anxiety may be worse.

performance, and overall life quality. In extreme cases, the problem can even increase the person's risk for depression, substance use disorder, and suicide.

It is important to have patience with the treatment process. It takes people different amounts of time to make progress. Some young people notice improvement after just a few weeks of treatment for anxiety, while others may need a few months. Others may take even longer to improve. What matters most is that the patient understands that anxiety treatment is not a race. A successful treatment is often defined as being able to manage anxiety rather than being completely anxiety-free.

Like other mental health disorders, an anxiety disorder comes with a possible risk for relapse. A person can overcome his or her anxiety at one point and then experience symptoms again at a later time. Some mental health professionals think the best way to help minimize the effects of a relapse is to make the patient aware that a relapse might take place. As psychologist Golda Ginsburg explained in an interview with the American Psychological Association (APA), checking in with the patient periodically might also help deter an anxiety disorder relapse, or at least lessen its negative effects. "In dentistry, we go for a checkup every six months," she pointed out. "We have 'well baby' checkups for kids. We don't do that in mental health, and I don't think that serves the families that need it. Waiting until there's a crisis and then going for help is problematic."[31]

A young person who shared their story anonymously on the NAMI website explained that for them, receiving a diagnosis of anxiety, depression, and obsessive-compulsive disorder (OCD) helped them make sense of the overwhelming feelings they had been dealing with for some time. Starting treatment, while difficult, was a light at the end of a long tunnel. They confronted their mental health issues with both honesty and hope.

"I'm always going to have these problems," they wrote, "but I am going to try my hardest to find the best ways to deal with them and fight through every day. Some days will be harder than others, and those are the days I will want to lie in bed and cry, but that's ok because some days I'll feel happy and those are the days that I will cherish."[32]

> "I'm always going to have these problems, but I am going to try my hardest to find the best ways to deal with them and fight through every day."[32]
>
> *—Anonymous anxiety sufferer*

SOURCE NOTES

INTRODUCTION: THE NAMELESS PROBLEM

1. Quoted in Susanna Schrobsdorff, "Teen Depression and Anxiety: Why the Kids Are Not Alright," *Time*, October 27, 2016. http://time.com.

2. Schrobsdorff, "Teen Depression and Anxiety: Why the Kids Are Not Alright."

3. Quoted in Schrobsdorff, "Teen Depression and Anxiety: Why the Kids Are Not Alright."

4. Richard Friedman, "The Big Myth About Teenage Anxiety," *New York Times*, September 7, 2018. www.nytimes.com.

CHAPTER 1: WHAT IS TEEN ANXIETY?

5. *Diagnostic and Statistical Manual of Mental Disorders* (*DSM–5*). Washington, DC: American Psychiatric Association Publishing, 2013.

6. Amy Morin, "10 Reasons Teens Have So Much Anxiety Today," *Psychology* Today, November 3, 2017. www.psychologytoday.com.

7. Sherri Gordon, "The Connection Between Bullying and Anxiety Disorders," *Verywell Family*, March 9, 2020. www.verywellfamily.com.

8. Quoted in Benoit Denizet-Lewis, "Why Are More American Teenagers Than Ever Suffering from Severe Anxiety?" *New York Times*, October 11, 2017. www.nytimes.com.

9. Sarper Taskiran, "Stigma Interferes with Mental Health Treatment for Kids," *US News & World Report*, July 24, 2018. http://health.usnews.com.

10. William Meek, "Overcoming Stigma for Generalized Anxiety Disorder," *Verywell Mind*, July 1, 2019. www.verywellmind.com.

CHAPTER 2: HOW DOES ANXIETY AFFECT TEENS?

11. Quoted in Julia Naughton, "This Is What I Live With: How Anxiety Affects the Everyday Life of One in Four Australians," July 15, 2016. www.huffingtonpost.com.au.

12. Quoted in Naughton, "This Is What I Live With."

13. Quoted in "Chronic Stress, Anxiety Can Damage the Brain, Increase Risk of Major Psychiatric Disorders," *ScienceDaily*, January 21, 2016. www.sciencedaily.com.

14. Quoted in Ana Sandoiu, "Boosting Brain's 'Executive Center' May Prevent Anxiety," *Medical News Today*, November 21, 2017. www.medicalnewstoday.com.

15. *Diagnostic and Statistical Manual of Mental Disorders* (*DSM–5*).

16. Desirae, "Empty and Anxious: Life with Anxiety," *National Alliance on Mental Illness,* n.d. www.nami.org.

17. Quoted in Lucy Dwyer, "When Anxiety Hits at School," *Atlantic*, October 3, 2014. www.theatlantic.com.

CHAPTER 3: HOW DOES TEEN ANXIETY AFFECT SOCIETY?

18. Quoted in Sid Lowe, "Bojan Krkic: 'I Had Anxiety Attacks, but No One Wants to Talk About That. Football's Not Interested," *Guardian*, May 18, 2018. www.theguardian.com.

19. Quoted in Lowe, "Bojan Krkic."

20. Saim Cheeda, "7 Ways Society Labels People with Anxiety Disorders," *Resources to Recover*, November 1, 2018. www.rtor.org.

21. Marwa Azab, "Inside the Thinking Maze of Anxious Minds," *Psychology Today*, April 13, 2018. www.psychologytoday.com.

22. "Teens Are Feeling More Anxious Than Ever," *Promises Behavioral Health,* July 2, 2013. www.promisesbehavioralhealth.com.

23. Quoted in Katie Lott, "Cady's Story: How One Teen Fought Anxiety," *Children's Wisconsin*, April 22, 2019. http://chw.org.

24. Clare Allan, "If We Hide Our Mental Issues, We Make It Easier for Society to Ignore Us," *Guardian*, March 14, 2017. www.theguardian.com.

25. Allan, "If We Hide Our Mental Issues, We Make It Easier for Society to Ignore Us."

SOURCE NOTES CONTINUED

CHAPTER 4: HOW CAN WE TREAT AND PREVENT TEEN ANXIETY?

26. Quoted in Alice Yin, "Coping with Teenage Anxiety: Readers Share Their Stories," *New York Times*, October 23, 2017. www.nytimes.com.

27. Jerry Bubrick, "Behavioral Treatment for Kids with Anxiety," *Child Mind Institute*, n.d. http://childmind.org.

28. Quoted in Yin, "Coping with Teenage Anxiety: Readers Share Their Stories."

29. Quoted in Gosia Wozniacka, "Mindfulness Training Helps Teens Cope with Stress and Anxiety," *Washington Post*, December 15, 2014. www.washingtonpost.com.

30. Lakshmy Nair, "How Exercise Improves Mood," *Livestrong.com*, August 24, 2018. www.livestrong.com.

31. Quoted in Kirsten Weir, "Brighter Futures for Anxious Kids," *American Psychological Association*, March 2017. www.apa.org.

32. "My Battle and Triumph Over OCD, Anxiety, and Depression," *National Alliance on Mental Illness,* n.d. www.nami.org.

FOR FURTHER RESEARCH

BOOKS

Jodi Aman, *Anxiety . . . I'm So Done with You*. New York: Skyhorse, 2020.

A.W. Buckey, *Dealing with Anxiety Disorder*. San Diego, CA: ReferencePoint Press, 2020.

Kate Frommer Cik, *Anxiety: The Ultimate Teen Guide*. Lanham, MD: Rowman and Littlefield, 2020.

Bitsy Kemper, *Teens and Phobias*. San Diego, CA: ReferencePoint Press, 2017.

Debra Kissen, *Rewire Your Anxious Brain for Teens*. Oakland, CA: New Harbinger Publications, 2020.

INTERNET SOURCES

Amy Ellis Nutt, "Why Kids and Teens May Face Far More Anxiety These Days," *Washington Post*, May 10, 2018. www.washingtonpost.com.

Marilyn Price-Mitchell, "Anxiety in Teens: How You Can Help," *Psychology Today*, November 30, 2019. www.psychologytoday.com.

Sarah Schuster, "22 Things People with Mental Illness Wish Their Parents Knew," *The Mighty*, March 17, 2016. www.themighty.com.

WEBSITES

National Alliance on Mental Illness
www.nami.org

The National Alliance on Mental Illness offers support and resources for teens who are looking to help themselves, a friend, or a loved one with mental health disorders, including anxiety.

Society for Adolescent Health and Medicine
www.adolescenthealth.org

The Society for Adolescent Health and Medicine provides mental health resources for teens and young adults.

TeenMentalHealth.org
http://teenmentalhealth.org

TeenMentalHealth.org aims to help improve the mental health of youth by providing information based on scientific evidence.

INDEX

INDEX CONTINUED

IMAGE CREDITS

Cover: © AntonioGuillem/iStockphoto
5: © Rawpixel.comShutterstock Images
7: © Monkey Business Images/Shutterstock Images
9: © vorDa/iStockphoto
11: © Adul10/Shutterstock Images
12: © Jacob Lund/Shutterstock Images
15: © Vgstockstudio/Shutterstock Images
18: © Red Line Editorial
20: © SeventyFour/Shutterstock Images
22: © twinsterphoto/iStockphoto
25: © file404/Shutterstock Images
27: © fizkes/iStockphoto
29: © Eraxion/iStockphoto
33: © Luis Molinero/Shutterstock Images
34: © Pormezz/Shutterstock Images
36: © Moore Media/iStockphoto
39: © Christian Bertrand/Shutterstock Images
41: © FluxFactory/iStockphoto
43: © Prostock-Studio/iStockphoto
44: © damircudic/iStockphoto
48: © FG Trade/iStockphoto
50: © shironosov/iStockphoto
53: © fizkes/iStockphoto
55: © SDI Productions/iStockphoto
58: © KatarzynaBialasiewicz/iStockphoto
60: © Pixel-Shot/Shutterstock Images
62: © FatCamera/iStockphoto
65: © SrdjanPav/iStockphoto
67: © MStudioImages/iStockphoto

ABOUT THE AUTHOR

Tammy Gagne has written dozens of books for both adults and children. Her recent titles include *What Is Gaming Disorder?* and *Dealing with Self-Injury Disorder*. She lives in northern New England with her husband, her son, and a menagerie of pets.